The Rainy Day Adventure

LITTLE TIGER PRESS

London

Little Elephant and Little Tiger were playing in the jungle, when suddenly,
SPLISH,
SPLOSH,
SPLASH,
it began to rain. "We'll have to shelter under that tree," said Little Tiger.

But Little Elephant was
too big. His front half
was dry, but his bottom
was still out in the rain!

He tried facing the other way.
Now his head was wet.
"Never mind," said Little Tiger.
"Let's go to the cave."

Little Tiger raced through the rain,
with Little Elephant splashing along
behind him.
"Nearly there!" shouted Little Tiger,
but when they arrived . . .

they found two bears.

"Go away!" shouted the biggest bear.
"We were here first."
Little Tiger didn't argue, because he
knew of somewhere even better.

They splashed through
the rain until they came
to a big rock.

Little Elephant squeezed under the rock
next to Little Tiger. But as he did, he
pushed Little Tiger out the other side.

"Thanks a lot, Little Tiger," said Little Elephant. "I'm dry at last."
"But I'm soaking wet," said Little Tiger. "Move up, Little Elephant!"
Little Elephant shifted his bottom and curled up his trunk, but there was still not enough room for the two of them.

They raced on until they
reached Little Tiger's
favourite fallen tree.

Little Tiger crawled underneath.
But poor Little Elephant couldn't
even get his head inside!

"Can't you think of anywhere else?" sniffed Little Elephant. He was very wet now.

"I know!" shouted Little Tiger. "We can shelter under the mango tree." But when they got there . . .

they found a family of monkeys
had already arrived.

"Come on in," chattered the
monkeys. "There's enough room."

But there wasn't enough room
for the monkeys as well.

"There's another cave by the river," said Little Tiger. So SPLISH, SPLOSH! Off they went to the river . . .

Suddenly Little Elephant skidded into Little
Tiger, and they both fell into the river.
"We're wetter than ever!" cried Little Elephant.

"It's fun though," said Little Tiger, and
they didn't even notice when the rain
stopped and the sun came out.

Written by Julie Sykes
Illustrated by Czes Pachela, based on the
characters created by Tim Warnes

LITTLE TIGER PRESS
An imprint of Magi Publications
1 The Coda Centre, 189 Munster Road, London SW6 6AW
www.littletigerpress.com
First published in Great Britain 2001
Text © 2001 Julie Sykes
Illustrations © 2001 Magi Publications
All rights reserved • Printed in Singapore • ISBN 1 85430 764 9
3 5 7 9 10 8 6 4 2